ALEXANDER GRAHAM *Bell*

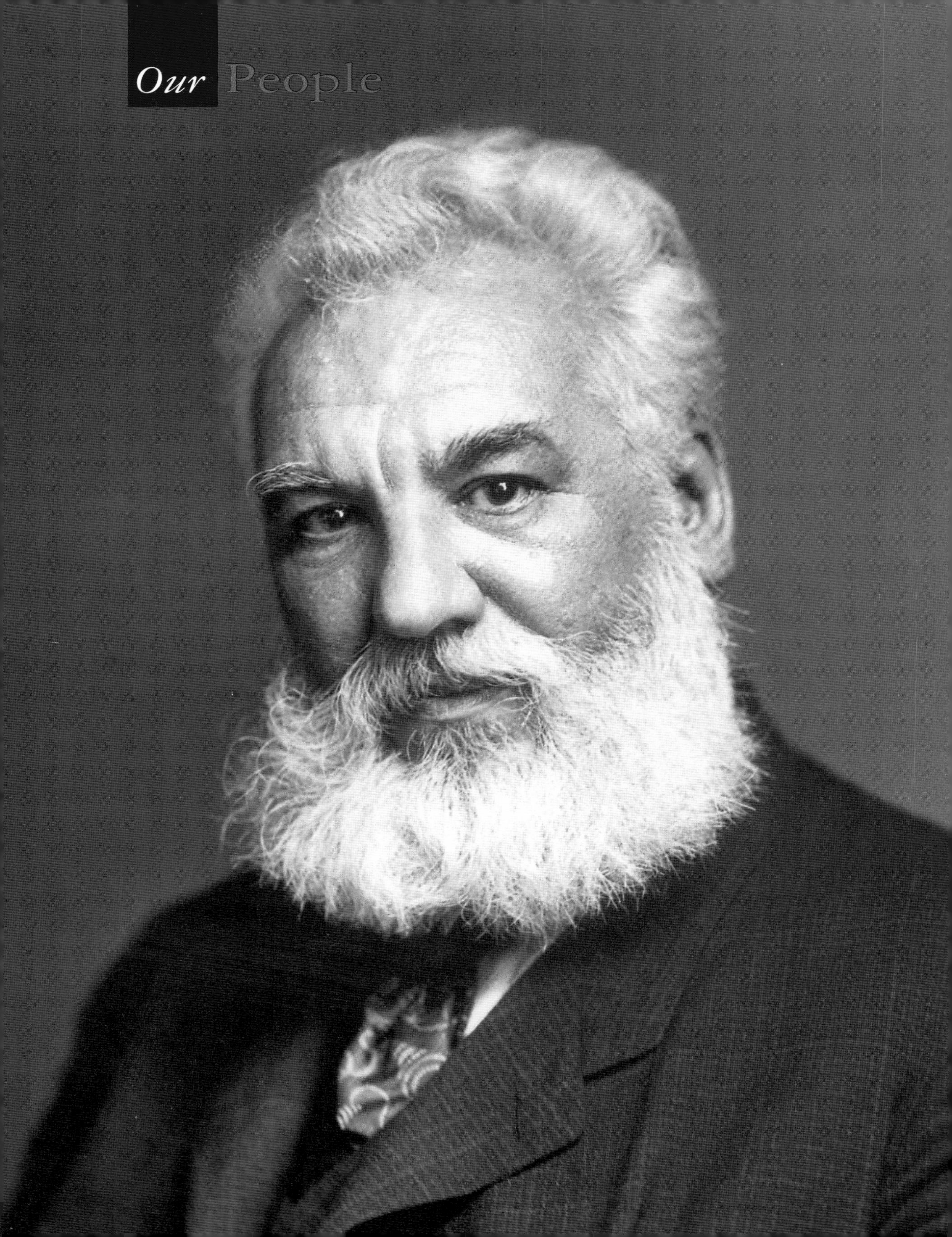
Our People

SPIRIT
of America®

ALEXANDER GRAHAM *Bell*

INVENTOR

By Cynthia Klingel and Robert B. Noyed

Content Adviser: Judith Tulloch, Historian, Parks Canada,
Atlantic Service Centre

The Child's World®
Chanhassen, Minnesota

7

ALEXANDER GRAHAM *Bell*

Published in the United States of America by The Child's World®
PO Box 326 • Chanhassen, MN 55317-0326 • 800-599-READ • www.childsworld.com

Acknowledgments
The Child's World®: Mary Berendes, Publishing Director

Editorial Directions, Inc.: E. Russell Primm, Emily J. Dolbear, and Pam Rosenberg, Editors; Dawn Friedman, Photo Researcher; Linda S. Koutris, Photo Selector; Sarah E. De Capua, Copy Editor; Susan Ashley, Proofreader; Tim Griffin, Indexer

Photo
Cover: Oscar White/Corbis; Parks Canada/Alexander Graham Bell National Historic Site of Canada: 22, 28; Corbis: 2, 21, 24, 25; Bettmann/Corbis: 6, 20; Sean Sexton Collection/Corbis: 9; Hulton-Deutsch Collection/Corbis: 13; Dave G. Houser/Corbis: 16; Library of Congress: 7, 8, 10, 12, 14, 17, 18, 19, 23, 26, 27.

Library of Congress Cataloging-in-Publication Data
Klingel, Cynthia Fitterer.
   Alexander Graham Bell, inventor / by Cynthia Klingel and
Robert B. Noyed.
      p. cm.
   "Spirit of America."
   Summary: A biography of the teacher and inventor best known
for his work with the deaf and his invention of the telephone.
   Includes bibliographical references and index.
   Contents: A family of educators—A growing interest—Inventing the telephone—
A successful life—Time line.
   ISBN 1-56766-367-2 (lib. bdg. : alk. paper)
   1. Bell, Alexander Graham, 1847–1922—Juvenile literature.
2. Telephone—History—Juvenile literature 3. Inventors—United
States—Biography—Juvenile literature. [1. Bell, Alexander
Graham, 1847–1922. 2. Telephone. 3. Inventors.] I. Noyed,
Robert B. II. Title.
TK6143.B4K57 2003
621.385'092—dc21
[B]

2002151667

20   25   27

Contents

Chapter ONE

A Family of Educators

Bell opens the telephone line providing service between New York and Chicago.

ALEXANDER GRAHAM BELL IS BEST KNOWN AS the inventor of the telephone. He also invented many other **devices** that helped people. Bell spent much of his life learning about speech and helping deaf people to speak.

Alexander Bell was born on March 3, 1847, in Edinburgh, Scotland. Alexander's parents, Alexander Melville and Eliza Grace Bell, did not give him a middle name when he was born. When he was about 11 years old, a family friend named Alexander Graham came to visit. Bell decided to use the name "Graham" as his middle name.

He then became known as Alexander Graham Bell. His family usually called him Alec, however.

Alexander's father was a professor of speech and elocution at Edinburgh University. Elocution is the art of public speaking. Bell's father was a speech expert. He was interested in helping people with speech and hearing difficulties.

Alexander's mother was a talented artist and musician who taught her sons how to play the piano. She was also deaf.

Alexander Graham Bell as a young boy

Alexander had two brothers. Eliza taught all of her sons at home. Alexander was a curious child who loved to read. He learned how to play the piano at a young age. When he was a child, he told his parents that he wanted to be a musician.

At the age of 11, Alexander began attending Royal Edinburgh High School. The school had many rules, which Alexander did not like. He studied Latin and Greek but was

Bell's grandfather had a great influence on his life.

not interested in most other subjects. He left the school after four years and never received his **diploma**.

Alexander also lived for a short time with his grandfather, Alexander Bell, in London, England. His grandfather had once taught speech and elocution at St. Andrews Grammar School. Later he moved to London to open a speech school. Alexander's grandfather was **strict** with his grandson and wanted him to study every day.

Alexander loved and admired his grandfather. While he was living with him, Alexander became more interested in speech. He learned a lot from his grandfather about the human voice.

After a year in London, Alexander Graham Bell returned to Edinburgh to live with his family. Bell did voice experiments with his dog. He trained the dog to growl on command. When the dog growled, Bell moved the dog's mouth and throat. These movements made it sound as if the dog was speaking!

Alexander also began working with his brother on a talking machine. They used a tin tube, a wooden box, cotton, and rubber. When they blew through the tube, they could make the machine say "Mama" in a high-pitched voice. They shared this invention with many of their friends. Alexander Graham Bell's interest in speech and language grew as he became an adult.

The Bell family lived in Edinburgh, Scotland until 1865.

A GROUP OF 33 MEN MET ON JANUARY 13, 1888, TO DISCUSS FORMING a "society for the increase and **diffusion** of geographical knowledge." They met several times over the next two weeks, and on January 27, 1888, the National Geographic Society was created. At that time, people were still exploring the unmapped western part of the United States. The society wanted to provide a way for Americans to learn about the country's geography.

Alexander Graham Bell's father-in-law, Gardiner Greene Hubbard (right), was the society's first president. He was a lawyer and **financier**. By electing him the first president, the members of the National Geographic Society made it known that a person did not have to be a geographer to be a member. Anyone with an interest in learning more about the world and sharing that knowledge with others was welcome. The second president was Alexander Graham Bell.

The society decided to publish a magazine to share this new information. They called it *National Geographic*. This famous magazine is still popular today. Over the years, the society has sponsored more than 4,000 research projects and expeditions. It publishes several magazines for adults and children. It also produces CD-ROMS and many television programs. The National Geographic Society even has its own television channel called the National Geographic Channel. Today, more than 10 million people who live in about 185 countries around the world are members of the National Geographic Society.

Chapter TWO

A Growing Interest

Bell was 18 years old when this picture was taken.

WHEN ALEXANDER GRAHAM BELL WAS ABOUT 15 years old, he took a job as a teacher at Weston House Academy, near Edinburgh. He taught music and speech there. Bell was younger than many of his students. He taught at the school for one year. Then he went to Edinburgh University to study Latin and Greek.

When Bell was 18 years old, he returned to Weston. His interest in speech and voice continued to grow. He learned more about how sound is created by experimenting with the **vibrations** in his throat and cheeks when he spoke.

The Bell family moved to London in 1865.

In 1865, Bell's grandfather died. Bell's father decided to continue his father's work and moved the family to London.

At that time, Alexander Melville Bell was working on a special kind of alphabet. After more than fifteen years of work, he finally finished an alphabet called Visible Speech. The Visible Speech system used symbols to

Bell also worked at the Pemberton Square School for the Deaf in Boston, Massachusetts.

stand for certain sounds. People who were deaf or had speech difficulties could use this alphabet to communicate.

In 1868, Alexander Graham Bell enrolled as a student at University College in London. He studied **anatomy** and **physiology**. He wanted to learn how the human body creates sound. At the same time, he began teaching deaf children how to use Visible Speech and read lips.

14

It was around this time that tragedy struck the Bell family. In 1867, Bell's younger brother Edward died of tuberculosis, a disease that affects the lungs. He was just 17 years old. About three years later, Bell's older brother Melville died of the same disease. Bell's father decided to move the family to Canada to protect the health of the rest of the family.

Shortly after the family arrived in Canada, Alexander Graham Bell moved to Boston, Massachusetts. He took a job teaching at a school for the deaf. He taught the Visible Speech system and worked hard to develop other methods of teaching. During the day, Bell was busy with his work as a teacher. At night, he worked to make a better electric telegraph. At that time, the telegraph could send only one message at a time. Bell wanted to design a machine that could read and send several messages at the same time. He called his idea the "harmonic telegraph."

Bell spent more than a year making his idea work. By the end of 1872, he was exhausted and returned to Canada to visit his parents.

Bell lived his adult life in the United States. However, he spent a lot of time in Nova Scotia, Canada, where he had a large estate in the town of Baddeck. The Canadian government opened the Alexander Graham Bell National Historic Site (below) to honor Bell and his work.

The Alexander Graham Bell National Historic Site has the largest and most complete collection of Bell's work in the world. There are replicas, or exact copies, of his inventions. **Artifacts** and documents help visitors understand Bell's life and work.

Many researchers visit the Alexander Graham Bell National Historic Site to study Bell's work. There they can read his actual notes. Young visitors to the site repeat Bell's experiments in the children's program.

Visitors to the Alexander Graham Bell National Historic Site also may be interested in traveling to Brantford, Ontario. There they can visit the Bell Homestead (above). This Canadian National Historic Site contains Melville House, the Bell family's first North American home. The house is furnished with a large collection of Bell family furniture and belongings. Visitors can see what life was like for the Bell family in the 1870s.

Chapter THREE

Inventing the Telephone

Mabel Hubbard as a child

IN 1873, ALEXANDER GRAHAM BELL BEGAN TO teach vocal physiology—how the human body produces spoken sounds—at Boston University. He also continued to work with deaf students.

Thomas Sanders was a wealthy businessman whose son George was born deaf. Sanders asked Bell to work with his son. Bell was also asked to work with Mabel Hubbard, the daughter of Gardiner Hubbard, an attorney in Boston. Bell had great success teaching Georgie and Mabel. Thomas Sanders and Gardiner Hubbard would have an important role in Bell's future.

One day in 1875, Bell went to an electrical shop to buy some equipment for his telegraph. He met a young man who worked at the shop named Thomas Watson. Watson soon began working with Bell on his experiments.

Sanders and Hubbard became interested in Bell's experiments. They gave Bell money to hire Watson and buy needed equipment. In time, Bell and Watson had great success with the telegraph and several other inventions. Bell wanted to design a speaking telegraph, or telephone. He had to develop a way to turn sound waves into electricity. One idea was to put a thin sheet of paper in the mouthpiece. He used an **electromagnet** to turn the sound vibrations into electricity. At the receiver end, a similar device turned the electricity back into sound.

With Watson's help, Bell had finally developed his design for the telephone. On March 7, 1876, he was granted a **patent** for his invention. The patent said Bell was the

Thomas Watson was Bell's assistant and one of his business partners.

19

THIS MODEL OF BELL'S FIRST TELEPHONE IS A DUPLICATE OF THE INSTRUMENT THROUGH WHICH SPEECH SOUNDS WERE FIRST TRANSMITTED ELECTRICALLY, 1875.

A model of Bell's first telephone

official inventor of the telephone. Bell was not finished with his work, however. He wanted his telephone to transmit sound more clearly.

Three days after Bell got his patent, he was testing the telephone **transmitter**. Wires connected the transmitter to the receiver, which was in the next room where Watson was working. When Bell spilled a bottle of acid on his trousers, he shouted into the transmitter, "Mr. Watson, come here, I want to see you." Bell was surprised when Watson came into the room and told him he heard Bell's voice through the receiver. It was the first telephone call!

Bell and Watson took turns making calls with the new invention. The sounds were fuzzy at first but became easier to understand. Bell had made a wonderful discovery. He now had to convince other people that his telephone would change the world.

Bell and Watson examine the first telephone.

IN 1885, THE BELL FAMILY WENT ON A TRIP TO NEWFOUNDLAND. Bell's father-in-law suggested they spend some time in Cape Breton in Nova Scotia. While there, Bell explored a village named Baddeck. Bell fell in love with the small village, the scenery, and the people. It all reminded him of his native Scotland. He recalled the many happy vacations he had spent in Scotland.

Bell purchased an estate in Baddeck called Beinn Bhreagh (BEN VREE-ah), which means "Beautiful Mountain" in Gaelic, the language of Scotland. The family first lived in a 13-room house called the Lodge.

The children had a small playhouse they called the Pansy Lodge.

In 1893, a large new house was built. It was called Beinn Bhreagh Hall. It had 11 fireplaces, a glassed-in porch, a stone terrace, a tennis court, and a stone **observatory**. There was even a laboratory for Bell.

Bell spent a lot of time at Beinn Bhreagh. His experiments in aeronautics, the science of designing and building aircraft, took much of his time there. While he worked, his wife Mabel was involved in the daily life of the village. She helped create the village library and started a reading club for young women. The Bells contributed a lot to the village, both financially and socially.

Beinn Bhreagh is still owned by Bell family members and is not open to the public. Alexander Graham Bell and Mabel Bell are both buried on the grounds of their beloved home.

Chapter FOUR

A Successful Life

Bell demonstrates his phone in 1877.

THE INVENTION OF THE TELEPHONE CHANGED forever the way people communicate. In June 1876, the Centennial Exhibition was held in Philadelphia, Pennsylvania. It celebrated the 100th anniversary of the founding of the United States. Bell brought his telephone to the exhibition. It earned the interest of many people, as well as a medal.

Bell was asked to travel throughout the country showing people how to use the telephone. The first outdoor telephone line was installed on April 4, 1877.

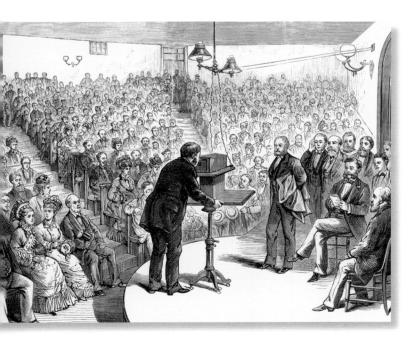

24

On July 9, 1877, the Bell Telephone Company was founded. Bell, Watson, Thomas Sanders, and Gardiner Hubbard and his daughter Mabel were founding members of the new company. The company began to make and sell telephones.

Two days after the company was founded, Bell married Mabel Hubbard on July 11, 1877. They had been friends for several years. When they were married, Bell was 30 years old and Mabel was 19. The couple later had two daughters.

Mabel and Alexander Graham Bell were friends for several years before they married.

The telephone—and the Bell Telephone Company—were very successful. Bell became a wealthy man, but he had no time to work on his many other inventions. So in 1880, he left the Bell Telephone Company. He was only 32 years old.

In 1880, Alexander Graham Bell won France's Volta Prize for scientific achievement in electricity. He used the money from the prize to set up the Volta Laboratory in Washington, D.C. He wanted it to be a place where inventors could carry out their work.

In 1881, Mabel Bell gave birth to a son. Sadly, the baby died from lung problems after a few hours. This tragedy inspired Bell to invent a vacuum jacket—a device that forced

The main reading room in the Volta Laboratory and Bureau building in Washington, D.C.

Bell (left) and his assistants observe the flight of his tetrahedral kite in 1908.

air into a person's lungs. His invention led to other inventions that worked better.

In 1885, Bell bought a house on an island in Nova Scotia, Canada. The Bell family spent their summers at the house. Bell built a workshop on the island so he could work on his inventions. He continued to work on many inventions for the rest of his life.

One of Bell's interests was making a flying machine. He designed and tested many different machines and kites. In 1903, the Wright Brothers successfully flew the first airplane. This event did not keep Bell from working on his planes and kites. Bell and some friends later created a plane that flew more than half a mile (0.8 kilometers).

Interesting Fact

▶ The Smithsonian Institution in Washington, D.C., has more than 150 pieces in an exhibit about Bell and the first telephones.

▶ Today's cellular phones, lasers, and fiber optics are based on Bell's early invention of the photophone, a device that uses a beam of light to transmit sound.

Bell continued to work on his inventions until his death on August 2, 1922. He was 75 years old. On the day of his funeral, all telephones throughout the United States were silent for one minute to honor the great inventor. Mabel, deeply saddened by her husband's death, died five months later.

The Bell Telephone Company, now known as American Telephone and Telegraph, or AT&T, still exists. It is hard to imagine life without the telephone. Alexander Graham Bell's invention truly changed communication throughout the world forever.

Many people attended the funeral of Alexander Graham Bell.

1847   Alexander Bell is born in Edinburgh, Scotland on March 3.

1858   Bell adopts the middle name "Graham" in honor of a family friend named Alexander Graham.

1862   Bell moves to London to spend a year with his grandfather.

1863   Bell begins teaching at Weston House Academy.

1865   Bell's grandfather dies. The family moves to London.

1867   Edward Bell, Alexander Graham Bell's brother, dies of tuberculosis.

1868   Bell begins taking classes at University College in London.

1870   Melville Bell, Alexander's older brother, dies of tuberculosis. The Bell family moves to Canada.

1871   Bell moves to Boston and begins teaching at the Boston School for Deaf Mutes.

1872   Bell meets Gardiner Greene Hubbard, a Boston attorney.

1873   Bell teaches at Boston University. Mabel Hubbard becomes one of his students.

1875   Thomas Watson begins working with Bell on his experiments.

1876   Bell is granted the patent for his telephone on March 7. He demonstrates the telephone at the Philadelphia Centennial Exhibition on June 25.

1877   Bell, Watson, Hubbard, and Sanders form the first telephone company on July 9. They call it the Bell Telephone Company. Bell and Mabel Hubbard are married two days later.

1880   Bell receives the Volta Prize from the French government.

1898   Bell is elected president of the National Geographic Society.

1922   Alexander Graham Bell dies.

1923   Mabel Hubbard Bell dies.

anatomy (eh-NAT-eh-mee)
Anatomy is the study of the structure of humans, animals, or plants. Bell studied human anatomy.

artifacts (AR-ti-faktz)
Artifacts are tools and objects used in the past. Museums contain many artifacts.

devices (dih-VICE-ez)
Devices are pieces of equipment that do specific jobs. The transmitter is a device that sends sound over wires to another device called a receiver.

diffusion (dif-YOO-zhen)
Diffusion is the spread of something, like an idea, from one group of people to another. The National Geographic Society was formed for the diffusion of geographic knowledge.

diploma (di-PLOH-mah)
A diploma is a certificate given to a person who graduates from a school. Alexander Graham Bell left high school without receiving his diploma.

electromagnet (ih-lek-troh-MAG-net)
An electromagnet is a magnet that becomes stronger when electricity passes through it. Bell used an electromagnet to turn sound vibrations into electricity.

financier (fin-an-SIR)
A financier is a person who works at raising and investing large amounts of money. Bell's father-in-law was a financier.

observatory (ub-ZUR-va-tor-ee)
An observatory is a building that contains scientific instruments for making observations. Museums called planetariums often have an observatory with telescopes for studying the planets and stars.

patent (PAT-nt)
A patent is a document that says a certain person or company is the only one with the right to make or sell an invention for a certain number of years. Alexander Graham Bell was given a patent for his telephone.

physiology (fiz-ee-OL-uh-jee)
Physiology is the study of how living bodies work. Bell studied human physiology.

strict (STRIKT)
To be strict means to make sure other people follow rules and behave well. Bell's grandfather was strict and made sure that Bell studied every day.

transmitter (trans-MIT-ur)
A transmitter is a piece of equipment that sends sounds to a receiver. Wires may connect the transmitter to the receiver.

vibrations (vy-BRAY-shunz)
Vibrations are rapid back-and-forth movements. Bell would touch his throat when he spoke to feel the vibrations of his vocal cords.

For Further INFORMATION

Web Sites

Visit our homepage for lots of links about Alexander Graham Bell:
http://www.childsworld.com/links.html

Note to Parents, Teachers, and Librarians:
We routinely verify our Web links to make sure they're safe,
active sites—so encourage your readers to check them out!

Books

MacLeod, Elizabeth. *Alexander Graham Bell: An Inventive Life.* New York:
Kids Can Press, 1999.

Sherrow, Victoria. *Alexander Graham Bell.* Minneapolis: Carolrhoda, 2001.

Shuter, Jane. *Alexander Graham Bell.* Chicago: Heinemann Library, 2000.

Places to Visit or Contact

Alexander Graham Bell National Historic Site of Canada

To find out more about the life and work of Alexander Graham Bell
P.O. Box 159
Baddeck, Nova Scotia
Canada
B0E 1B0
902/295-2069

National Museum of American History
Smithsonian Institution

To see the exhibit Information Age: People, Information & Society
14th Street and Constitution Avenue, N.W.
Washington, DC 20013-7012
202/357-2700

Index